Tomoiya's Story

Escape To Darkness

By

C. A. King

Cover Design: SelfPubBookCovers.com/Ravenborn

Dedication And Acknowledgement Page

This book is dedicated to readers everywhere. Without you,
my novels would be nothing more than words on a blank page
-and-
To all participants of
NaNoWriMo
for their support and motivation throughout the years
-and-
To the elephant, otter and other critter pictures
that brighten our days and make us call for mattresses
to support the 'Thud'.

Look for other Books by C.A. King including:
The Portal Prophecies:
Book I - A Keeper's Destiny
Book II - A Halloween's Curse
Book III – Frost Bitten
Book IV - Sleeping Sands
Book V – Deadly Perceptions
Book VI – Finding Balance

Copyright Page

This book is a work of fiction. Any historical references, real places. real events, or real persons names and/or persona are used fictitiously. All other events, places, names and happenings are from the author's imagination and any similarities, whatsoever, with events both past and present, or persons living or dead, are purely coincidental.

Copyright © 2016 by C .A. King

All rights reserved. This book or any portion thereof may not be reproduced or used in any manner whatsoever without the express written permission of the author and/or publisher except for the use of brief quotations in a book review or scholarly journal.

Cover Design: SelfPubBookCovers.com/Ravenborn

First Printing: 2016

ISBN 978-1-988301-08-2

Kings Toe Publishing
kingstoepublishing@gmail.com
Burlington, Ontario. Canada

Prologue

The universe - it surrounds us. Never ending. Never dying. It goes on even when its inhabitants don't. People sit in their cozy homes thinking the minuscule bubble of existence that surrounds them is all there is - completely self-absorbed by their own egos. If only they knew how wrong they are. Each time someone thinks they have solved all the mysteries, someone else finds even more waiting for an answer. Sometimes, our universe is forced to expand. There is no choice but to venture forward - leap into unknown. Sometimes, that's where individual stories begin.

Space travel. *To some, it is an advancement; a way to meet new races, learn new traditions; explore new cultures - a chance to expand the mind with knowledge of the unknown. To others, it is nothing more than a new outlet of resources to exploit and destroy. To the naive and trusting, it is a recipe for disaster. The question of whether or not venturing into the realm of the stars is worthwhile, is a topic that will be argued for generations to come.*

Chapter One

A single star - nothing more than a speck of light against a backdrop of darkness. To the naked eye, it remained the same - a constant. *Sight can lie.* Travelling in space at a fast velocity meant that lone star loitered in the confines of a part of the universe she left behind. Along the way, new stars replaced it. The process had already repeated thousands of times since the sparkling light first caught her attention. The mind - throughout time has always been a fragile thing - coping with anomalies that it wasn't able to wrap itself around by fooling the senses into believing something else to be truth.

Tomoiya's gaze shifted, fixating on the open space passing by at unfathomable speeds - the finest ship in her Father's fleet delivering her like a parcel into the unknown.

Until today, her universe consisted of what she now thought of as the light side. The suns for each galaxy burnt brightly, in different hues of yellow, white and orange including the golden sun, currently providing heat and light to her own world. Now, reality had been shattered.

It was only this morning when she first heard about another part of the universe - a darker side. The suns there cast rays made up of shadows, tinted in blues, purples and reds. The circumstances of the past few days left her no choice but to head into the dark. As long as threats existed, the unknown would hail to home.

Her grip on the book, *Allaynie's Story*, tightened, putting pressure on its frail bindings, already worn from time. What was once her mother's prized possession now fell to Tomoiya to care for. Wrinkles on her face formed, showing signs of the turmoil twisting her insides - tying them into knots.

Who forgets their own mother?

The details of years passed fogged her memory like steam on glass. Every picture, card, or other remembrance of the woman, was now sealed away in a box, safely hidden on the top shelf of her closet. Everything, that is, except the one book.

There wasn't even a trace of doubt in Tomoiya's mind that the two of them spent many sleepless nights together reading from it. Years passed and the journal now served as a connection to what she couldn't remember.

No complaints. She enjoyed reading the carefully-crafted words. Written by a young girl named Allaynie, in a time long forgotten, the novel was a dairy of her adventures - chronicling a time of peace and happiness.

"Allaynie's Story," a man's voice said. He sat across from her. "That was always one of your favourites."

Tomoiya nodded. Enough had transpired in the past few days that she simply didn't feel like talking. It has been said that it's best to speak about things - get them off one's chest. She didn't agree. Talking would only bring out the emotions - the tears she fought so hard to hold back.

"Do you know what happens to her?" The man asked. "To Allaynie?"

Tomoiya shook her head.

The man smiled. "Would you like to know? I can't promise a happy ending, but I think it may help you understand things better."

"Was she real?" Tomoiya asked, her voice only slightly louder than a whisper.

"Yes," the man answered. "She was real." He leaned back in the reclining chair, crossing his legs. Even if he couldn't take her gaze from the cold space whirling by them, at least he caught her interest.

This was a story someone else should have told her - her father, ideally. There was no time for that now. She needed to know how the familiar tale ended. Her fate and Allaynie's were intricately woven together. They were so similar. Hopefully, they wouldn't share the same destiny. If she was to have any chance at happiness, she needed to know how this story ended - to try to avoid making similar mistakes.

"The book ends on the day Allaynie is to be blood wed," Tomoiya said. "I always assumed the marriage was where she decided to end her adventures. It seemed like a good place - you know - and they lived happily ever after."

The man took the book from her. He flipped through the aged sheets preserved by the finest bookkeepers in their kingdom. "Yes. I agree," he said. In the past, the familiar words that graced its pages passed through his lips on countless story nights. He didn't blame her for not remembering now. The death of her mother created a mental block no one had been able to shatter. It wasn't unusual for a young child to put up defences against something as painful as losing a parent.

"Tell me," Tomoiya said, leaning back in her chair.

"As you wish," he answered. "Once upon a time, in a kingdom far, far away..."

"You're kidding, right?" Tomoiya smirked at the man's storytelling abilities. She wasn't a little girl anymore. She knew fairy tales weren't real. There was a time when she waited for her prince in shining armour to ride up and whisk her away. He never came. In fact, she hadn't even met a boy she considered being more than just friends with. For the past few years, she watched her friends find boys to date. She winced at the thought of her friend. The gruesome murder she witnessed played back like a movie in her head.

"Who is the one telling this story?" he asked, snapping her back to reality.

That was what she needed - something a little more jovial to make her forget. She pressed her lips together tightly, but not even that could hide the smirk starting to form. Her finger pointed at the man.

"That's right," he said. "And who is the one listening?"

Her finger curled back towards herself.

"Glad we established that," he said. "Can we continue?"

She nodded.

"Once upon a time, in a kingdom far, far away..."

Chapter Two

The two glass doors to the balcony swung open. Red chiffon curtains, caught in the gusty wind, blew freely. Allaynie laughed. The cool feel of the window coverings tickled the skin on her arms, sending a shivering sensation down her spine. She danced with the wind as if it had been her partner for many years.

"What in the universe are you doing?" Her mother asked.

"Dancing," Allaynie replied. A gust of wind grabbed the material from her hands, arching it up over her head. It fell down, forming a veil over her golden hair. "Appropriate - don't you think?" she mused.

"You have a proper wedding veil in your room," her mother answered. "I think I'd prefer if you wore it instead of the window coverings."

"I think she looks perfect."

"You're biased," her mother teased, paying little attention to the man who entered the room.

"Of course I am," he answered. "Not only is she my daughter, she is also princess of this magnificent world. There isn't a living thing that could come close to your beauty." His lips brushed the side of her face with affection. "You will make the perfect bride. I hope that young man knows exactly how lucky he is."

She giggled. "He does," she said. "He has every intention of making me the happiest girl alive." The cushion bounced as she plopped down beside her mother.

"Yes. Well, keep in mind it isn't too late to have a change of heart," the king declared. "I have no issues calling off the whole thing right now. You do have other suitors. What about Bantil? You turned him down rather hastily, if you ask me. Perhaps, you should take some time and reconsider."

"Bantil has always been good to me, but I am not in love with him," Allaynie answered.

The queen sighed. "You have to let her grow up. She can't remain your little girl forever."

"Indeed," her father agreed. "But a little longer wouldn't hurt."

"I suppose it's time for me to dress," her mother cooed. "The guests will be arriving soon. I have details to go over."

Details were something the queen adored. The stress of perfection suited her personality. Allaynie smiled, knowing every last flower would be placed with the same style and flair that she had become accustomed to throughout her life. Nothing would be overlooked. Her wedding would be flawless - the envy of all.

"Have you seen my future husband?" Allaynie asked.

"Some strangers arrived earlier this morning," the king answered, gazing out the window at the scurrying workers setting up tables and chairs. "He went to extend an invitation to join in the festivities."

Allaynie linked her arm in her father's. Resting her head against him, she joined his surveillance of the preparations underway two storeys below. "I hope they accept," she said. "I want as many people as possible to join in my joy."

Her father chuckled. "They will, my dear. This will be the happiest day of your life - that, I promise."

Chapter Three

"Welcome," Mijellin exclaimed. The fabric of his red velvet jacket wrinkled upwards, tugged by the motion of his outstretched arms. "What brings travellers to our world from afar?"

"Merely a stop over," the captain answered. "We miscalculated our needs and are in hope of finding a few supplies. I am known as Woden." His fingers grasped tightly around the rim of his oval-shaped hat adorned with a brightly coloured plume, removing it in the same motion as his bow. Pieces of his long hair came loose from the blue ribbon that was meant to hold them in place, revealing a circular bald spot.

"And I am Mijellin," the prince answered, mimicking the same gesture. "You have come on the most fortunate of occasions, as it is my wedding day. I extend an invitation to your entire crew to join in the festivities."

"That is a most generous offer," Woden said. "We have journeyed far. The men will be excited to take a day to celebrate with your family, although we have no gift prepared." He motioned to his lead hand to inform the rest of the crew.

"No gift is necessary," Mijellin blurted out. He threw his arm around the shoulder of the captain. "We are most grateful to have more people celebrate our expression of love. Come. Let me introduce you to the rest of my family."

A young man ran forward. Bowing his head, he left both hands open in front of him to take the captain's hat and well-worn brown jacket.

"Thank you," Woden muttered, hesitating to remove his coat. He sighed and pulled it off, revealing a holster holding several weapons.

"My goodness," Mijellin said. "You are well-equipped. You won't be needing any of those this evening."

"Not all places are as hospitable as your world," The captain stated. "There have been times where self-defence has been necessary. I assure, you it's mainly for show." The corners of his slightly parted lips pushed upwards forming a rather unnerving smile. The metals, now making their homes where teeth had once resided, glimmered. "I hope we haven't taken you away from your bride to greet us," Woden offered, attempting to change the topic.

"No," the prince replied. "Not at all. The ceremony won't start for a few hours."

Woden's eyes glanced around at the scenery. "That's rather late for such an important event - isn't it?" he asked. It only made sense that a civilized world such as this would begin a wedding ceremony during the day.

"Late," Mijellin laughed. "It's only mid-morning. I think space fatigue has gotten the better of you, my friend." He slapped the captain on the back before picking up the pace again.

Woden snickered under his breath. For morning, this world was dimly lit. He glanced up at the sky. A full laugh escaped from his lungs. What he mistook for a red moon was actually this world's sun. He shook his head. The journeys he embarked on led him to all sorts of wonders, but never before to a planet of darkness. He added a skip to his step, catching up to his host in time to see him kiss a woman of incredible beauty on her cheek. His gaze lingered over the woman's curves, tracing each one in his mind. His tongue darted out, licking his lips - an effect of admiring her porcelain white skin accentuated by high cheekbones and glowing mauve eyes.

"Captain," Mijellin said. "May I introduce my future mother-in-law, Queen Claudette."

Woden bowed, placing one arm over the missing button of his white shirt. "Madam," he flirted. "May I be so bold as to say your world is the luckiest I have found in all my travels to have a woman as elegant and graceful as yourself for its queen."

Claudette muffled a giggle. "You sir," she said, "have a silver tongue - not that I am complaining. Compliments make the universe a nicer place." She patted her white hair neatly twisted into a braided up-do - a reaction to the stranger's words rather than a need to flatten rogue strands of hair. She kept her appearance meticulous at all times. Not even a single hair would dare defy her standards.

"Indeed they do, m'lady," Woden answered. "When they are sincere. I'm afraid there are no words that I can find that could do you justice."

Her arm snaked around his, directing him to a table. "You'll have a perfect view from these seats," the queen said. "Feel free to ask for food or drink at any time. The wait staff will attend to whatever your wish." Her hands smoothed over the cream-coloured dress that cloaked her body. "Other guests are beginning to arrive. I hope we have a chance to speak again later."

"I'll be taking my leave as well," Mijellin announced. "Enjoy the festivities, my new friends."

Woden bowed his head.

"I didn't know you was such an upstanding citizen, Cap'n," His lead hand mocked - the crew cackling behind him.

Woden's stomach popped out into a jiggling mass - his skin visible in the gap where a button, now missing, had once hinged his shirt together. "Sit down," he commanded, slouching into a chair of his own. "It would do some good if the lot of you showed a little class tonight." An old piece of food lodged between his teeth loosened. His tongue wiggled it around for a bit. Giving up, he made a smacking noise - sucking it free before spitting it out. "Normally I would have ate that," he grunted. "Things aren't going well for us at the moment."

Silence fell over the table. A young waiter poured red liquid into crystal chalices sitting before each of the men. Woden watched as he disappeared to attend to other duties.

"That journalist messed us up," he continued. "I don't know how she got those pictures of us killing that big cat, Manny, but it's dried up all of our business." He sighed. "It was once a sign of status to wear the fur of an animal no one else had, or eat the flesh of a beast so rare it may never be tasted again. Now, everyone is scared of what it will do to their reputations to be caught. That article called us nothing more than glorified poachers destroying the universe. I'd like to skin that woman alive."

He swirled the red liquid around in the glass before taking a large mouthful and gulping it back. Using his arm for a sleeve, he wiped his mouth. "I'd prefer ale," he chuckled. "But, beggars can't be choosers. We have a full meal coming and all the wine we can drink." He lifted his glass making a cheers motion to his men before finishing off its contents.

"We're getting the meal no matter how we act," Manny scoffed. "These folks are too fancy to kick us out and make a big scene."

"Perhaps," Woden said, motioning for the waiter to return with more wine. "Leave the bottle, please. My friends and I are a bit thirsty." The young man nodded and complied. "If I play my cards right," Woden continued, "I think I can swindle the supplies we need to get us home from these babbling idiots."

His posture straightened. Sucking in his belly again, he waved one hand in a gesture of greeting to the queen as she passed by showing other guests to their seats.

A few men at the table snickered at the sight of their captain. "Quiet." Manny's fist smashed down, knocking over his glass. The red liquid spilled out, staining the crisp white linen that draped over the table. The spot grew bigger, resembling a pool of blood flowing from an open wound at a grisly murder scene.

"You idiot," Woden grunted, reaching to pick up the glass. "Don't just watch it."

A waiter ran over, rushing to attend to the spill before any of the other guests noticed the mess.

"I apologize for my friend," Woden offered.

"No problem, sir," the young waiter replied, replacing the chalice with a new one and filling it half way to the top. "If you need anything else, please let me know." He bowed before scurrying off to another table. The rich and famous of this world were arriving now - taking up much of the wait staff's attention.

"Cap'n," Manny said. "Have you noticed these folks all have odd coloured, glowing eyes and strange teeth?"

"Indeed I have," Woden admitted, his belly flapping back over his belt buckle again. "There is something not right about this bunch, but that doesn't mean we shouldn't accept their generosity." He held a bottle upside down over his glass, allowing the last of the red wine to trickle out, not wasting a drop. He motioned another cheers, freezing before his lips had the opportunity to feel the wetness they longed for. His gaze locked, captured by the palace he had previously never given any attention to. "Now who is that?" he asked, not wanting or expecting an answer.

The men followed his line of vision to a second-floor balcony. A woman dressed in a red off-the-shoulder gown graced the terrace with an angelic presence.

Chapter Four

Woden slouched in his seat. Tilting his head backwards, he threw a few berries in the air, catching them in his mouth on their way back down. His crew cheered at their leader's success. He smiled, chewing the fruit with his mouth open.

"Looks like they are ready to start," Manny pointed out.

A trumpet blew a loud declaration of commencement. The men side-eyed each other without words, snickering under their breath at the procession of men dressed in velvet jackets covering white ruffled shirts. There was no need to keep up appearances - all attention was on the show. He allowed his shoulders to haunch over, revealing the beginnings of a hump forming on his back. His elbow rested on the rear of his chair - two fingers in turn propping up his head. A thumb nail wedged between golden and silver, plaque-covered teeth.

Ceremony can bore a man to death.

"Sammy," Woden said without moving. "Pass the bottle." He outstretched his free hand, waiting for it to be filled.

Sammy, or more correctly Samson, was the largest member of the crew in both height and weight. His hair-covered arm spanned the table with ease, complying with his captain's wishes. As big as he was, he was also a man of few words, motioning towards the end of the procession with a nod.

The bottle slammed down on the table. She caught his attention - the woman in red from the balcony, gliding towards them. The slouch was gone. Woden rubbed the stubble under his mouth, his eyes never drifting from their current view. A single chuckle managed to escape the crooked half-smile formed by his closed lips. As if whisked away to another place, his eyes went dead. At that moment, every ounce of compassion they contained drained away.

Gold fever struck its target, piercing his heart and removing all traces of goodwill left.

Although everything about the woman screamed gold, it wasn't the highlights in her hair, the colour of her eyes or the shimmering radiance that coated her skin that Woden saw. It was the crown jewels that adorned her head, framing her face and neck.

"Gorgeous," he muttered. "I've never seen such stunning jewels. There may be more to this world than I anticipated."

"Aye," Manny agreed. "But we aren't thieves by trade."

"True," Woden replied. "But we are hunters. I am more than accustomed to taking home trophies." He threw his head back, emptying the remainder of the contents of his crystal chalice into his mouth. A gulp forced it down. A new decanter taunted him into pouring another glass.

The woman's gaze never faltered from a flower-covered archway positioned in the middle of a platform at the end of the aisle.

The bride - that could be a complication.

His attention turned to a winged bug, desperately trying to escape the red liquid swirling around like a whirlpool in his glass. He smiled. One finger swooped in and rescued it. Its tiny body struggled to recover on the white linen. A fist smashed down.

Mercy is for the weak and poor.

"What are they doing?" Manny asked, his face wrinkled with disgust. "Are they ... biting each other?"

Clapping and cheering.

The happy couple waved. Droplets of blood trickled from the corner of the bride's crimson lips almost matching their colour.

"I believe they were," Woden said.

A mouthful of wine lay beside Manny's hole-worn shoes. He spat several times, making sure every bit his pallet held was expelled.

Woden cackled. "I doubt there is any blood in the wine." He downed a full glass in one breath. "Still, things are beginning to feel more and more like a hunt is upon us." His eyes ogled the prize, visiting each table to collect congratulations. The cold sweat of anticipation left moisture on his brow. He closed his eyes, enjoying every second of the burst of adrenaline surging throughout his body. Hunting was his addiction and it offered a rush far better than any substance ever could.

A vision formed - a plan in its humble beginning form.

"Woden," Mijellin exclaimed, approaching the strangers. "I'd like you to meet my wife, Princess Allaynie."

"A pleasure," he offered, bowing his head. Wine doesn't mix well with trying to keep up appearances. Keeping his gut from jiggling like a bowl of jelly relied on how long he could hold in his breath. That, of course, was the only place on the captain that was out of shape, unless one counted his less than desirable posture. The contour of lean muscles on his legs and arms were undeniably present, showing through his clothing when he moved. "That was an interesting ceremony. I'm afraid we aren't familiar with your customs. Perhaps you have a moment to explain to us what we witnessed."

"We'd be happy to," the king bellowed, staggering. Wrapping an arm around the bride and groom, he wedged himself between them. His rosy cheeks and glazed over copper-tone eyes bore witness to the man's overindulgence in the evening's preferred drink. "My most beautiful daughter blood wed Mijellin a few moments ago."

"Blood wed?" Woden asked.

"Yes," the king answered. "I'll take that." He snatched a bottle off a passing silver tray. His overflowing chalice leaked stains down the front of the brightly coloured, silk robe that covered his normal regal attire. "More?" The bottle passed without incident to the captain.

"I am glad you could join us," Allaynie commented. "If you will excuse me, I believe my mother is waiting for me." She glanced back at her father, shaking her head. Hangover would be the word of the day tomorrow.

"What were we discussing?" the king asked. "Oh yes, I remember. The blood bond. You see in our world, every male is given a blood ring at birth. The ring grows with the boy, until the day he finds his soulmate, when it splits into two. The second part he places on the finger of his betrothed."

"How romantic," Woden said, forcing a smile.

Romance - the downfall of many a good man.

He pitied those who fell into the web of the black widows in society. His wife knew her place - at home, away from him. She bore him five offspring and that was enough. For her troubles, he paid the bills and kept her in spending money.

"At the wedding ceremony, the two exchange blood, which binds the ring to their fingers, and their souls together for eternity," The king choked on the last few words, sniffling back tears.

"When you say exchange blood," Woden said. "You mean drink it?"

"Well, of course," the king laughed. "What else would they do with it?"

"I apologize," Woden offered. "We are not familiar with your race. Does it have a name? We answer as the race of man."

"Vampire," The king bellowed. "We are the great race of vampires."

"Vampire," Woden repeated. "A new term for the great race of men."

"A toast," the king exclaimed. "To men and vampires. May they enjoy a long and fruitful friendship from this day forward." He lifted his cup slurping back the contents. "If you will excuse me, I see some people I haven't had a toast with as of yet. Enjoy the evening, my new comrades."

Mijellin laughed. "My father-in-law is relishing in the festivities a little too much," he said. "We don't often have many visitors. Space travel is so new to this part of the universe. I myself work on our own fleet, albeit not as advanced as the ship that carries you."

"You are interested in space travel?" Woden asked.

"Most certainly," Mijellin answered. "The elders may think it isn't necessary, but I can tell it will be the way of the future. Currently, we only use it to visit a few neighbouring worlds, but the time will come where we will find the need to go further out. I have been planning for that day. I have a gift for understanding the mechanics of how things work. I need only see the parts function as a whole and I can reconstruct it in record time."

"I would be happy to give you a tour of our vessel," Woden offered. "Perhaps you will find something that will help your quest for advancement in space travel. We have no secrets great enough to hide from new friends."

"A most generous offer. I would be most honoured," the newlywed responded. His neck stretched, looking for his bride. "I believe I can sneak away for a few minutes without being missed. Would now be alright?"

Bait acquired. Trap set.

Chapter Five

"M'lady," Woden whispered in the princess' ear. "There has been an accident. Your husband is injured. He requested I bring you immediately."

"Where?" Allaynie shrieked. "Show me."

Worry - it removes reasonable thought from existence.

"He was taking a tour of our vessel," the captain answered. "This way." His hand slipped into hers, leading her to his ship.

The lure was cast.

Her stride only faltered for a moment entering the spaceship. Space travel may have excited her husband, but it frightened her. There were some people who should never mingle with others.

She looked around, trying to make sense of her surroundings. Her gaze locked on the man she, only a few hours ago, wed - now covered in bruises, lying on the cold metal floor. "What happened?!" she screamed, kneeling by his side. Her hand ran over the swelling face of the man she loved.

The one eye he could open examined his bride. "Run," he whispered in a broken voice. His warning came too late. The only door back to her world came down with a crash.

Bait taken.

"Why are you doing this?" Allaynie screamed.

Woden circled her - stalking his prey. "Those are beautiful jewels. May I see them?" he asked, snatching the tiara from her head. A few golden strands came loose with it. "Extraordinary. I've never seen amber diamonds before."

"They are," she started, pausing for a moment. "Exclusive to this world. If that is what you want, take them."

Woden sidestepped an onslaught of jewels launched in his direction. "Thank you," he said, laughing. "But these aren't enough. Are there more?" He grabbed her by the arm, lugging her to her feet, only to shove her into a chair. "Get him to his knees."

"There are some," Allaynie answered. "But they are locked away in the palace. I can't access them tonight."

The captain nodded to Manny. A shiny, silver blade pressed against Mijellin's throat, cutting deep enough into skin to allow a trickle of blood to cascade the length of his neck before disappearing under his collar.

"Please!" she screamed - efforts to choke back tears failed. One single drop escaped the corner of her eye. It slid down her cheek before falling off her chin. A clang sounded as it hit the floor.

"What's this?" Woden asked, a perfectly formed teardrop diamond resting in the palm of his hand. He held it up to the light, examining it with one eye. A husky laugh escaped from somewhere deep inside the pit of his stomach. "It seems there are more. How ironic something so beautiful is born from tears of sadness. Kill him."

"Wait, please!" she shrieked. "I'll do anything."

Woden motioned to his lead hand to stop. "You agree to do what I say and I will let him live. Will you agree to belong to me?"

"No," Mijellin muffled, receiving a kick to his midsection for his efforts. Blood sputtered out onto the cold floor - a result of coughing.

"I will," she promised.

"Get him off my ship," the captain commanded. "Make sure he can't use his legs to find help. I'd rather not have to outrun anyone - even if their technology isn't as advanced as ours." A clang signalled the opening of the door.

Trophy acquired.

A metal container fell onto Allaynie's lap. A shiver traversed her spine - fear perhaps, or maybe it was the result of the cold sensation transferring from the smooth canister to her body. "What's this for?" she asked.

"To collect my fortune," the captain answered, grinning like a fairytale cat. "Cry."

"I can't cry on command," she pleaded.

"Then I guess I'll have to help you," Woden said, his belt already in his hand. "This will hurt you much more than me."

Face down on the ground, she squirmed an attempt to escape - the laughter of a madman ringing in her ears. The belt came down across exposed shoulder blades, with intense stinging pain on impact. Tension filled every muscle preparing for the next lash. She didn't have to wait long. Each time the leather strap made contact with her skin, it had a little more force behind it. She screamed - no one would hear.

Tears.

*****

"How is the princess today?" Woden asked, the pot of coffee in one hand filling a silver cup in the other. Metal touched his lips before the pot returned to its holder. A loud slurping noise followed by a smack of the lips accompanied every sip. "Strong and bitter," he said. "The way I like it."

"No movement from the girl," Manny answered. "Most likely she passed out from the pain some time during the night."

"What's the count?" A handful of golden tear shaped diamonds fell through the gaps between his fingers. His hand submerged, clenching another handful to repeat the process.

"Two hundred and eighty-two - not counting the jewelry she was wearing." Manny answered. "Enough to pay off the debts and have some in reserve - if we get a good price."

"I guess I can give her a day or two to recover," Woden said, walking over to the motionless body curled up in a ball. "I don't want to break our investment."

"Ugh," Allaynie muffled a cry. Guided by the pressure of a foot to her side, she rolled onto her stomach. A calloused hand ran across her exposed skin, pulling up bits of torn fabric where the leather strap and hit particularly hard. Laughter cut through any mental defences she had left. The belt made contact again. This time her captor used the buckle side.

"Looks like someone has healing abilities," Woden howled. "No need to wait to start another session to increase our wealth."

A few lashes brought only pleas for mercy. The undeniable crack of bone resonated in an almost musical rhythm from where the buckle hit, leaving a bloody imprint of an eagle behind. The intensity of the beating increased steadily without worry for her health. The physical wounds would heal - the mental scars multiplied.

Tears.

Chapter Six

There are questions in the universe that may never be answered. Whether or not a person has an infinite number of tears is one of them. Bodies adjust - evolve. Desensitized by pain - hers no longer caused her to wallow in self-pity. The river of wealth that flowed freely for the past month was drying up. The drought took its toll on the captain's newly-acquired lavish lifestyle.

He dug in his pocket for change, pulling out only a few pennies and an old button. He mused at the opalescent circle. A reminder of a way of life he vowed never to return to. He flipped the button with his thumb, catching it on the way back down. It popped off his shirt the day he arrived in a strange world. The day he acquired her as his trophy and meal ticket. He scoffed at the thought of her defiance. A way to break her would appear and he would make use of the opportunity with a smile on his face.

The corner of his eye caught a glimpse of today's newspaper. A picture of his son consorting with that woman displayed on the front page. He winced. That woman, Eva - the journalist that ruined his business, calling for an end to the horror of his hunting. That woman who had the audacity to call him a cold-blooded murderer.

There is a fine line between hunting game and murder. Isn't everyone a beast by nature?

Eva's voice was getting louder - stronger and with it came power. Her disagreement with the display of the vampire was front page news - questioning the morality of the conditions she was being kept in. He rubbed his fingers along the wrinkles on his forehead.

Worry lines. That journalist had caused them.

A task force was coming. Even his refusal to allow them access to her wouldn't matter in the end. They would come and snatch his trophy from under his nose.

Stupid people - why didn't they listen?

The attraction was a success at first. Families rushed in to see the caged beast that cowered away from sunlight and drank the blood of others from her fangs. The word vampire was an overnight success - a new monster for the modern age. The masses were eating it up and wanting more. All over the light side of the universe, books were being written and movies filmed - all about vampires. Some glorified them, but most called them monsters.

Who's the monster - man or beast?

If Allaynie talked, it was all over. His fist made contact with a wall leaving an indent. Blood trickled down his knuckles over bruises already forming. It swelled. He grabbed two ice cubes from the freezer contemplating using them on his hand. They clanged together in a glass instead. The best whiskey money could buy streamed over them, until each began to float. The first sip slid down his throat leaving a burning sensation along its path. "Ah." His lips pursed together.

Options - there had to be some.

Killing Allaynie outright would lead to too many questions. He was too far into the limelight - thanks to the reporter. Perhaps pressuring the vampire to keep silent might work. He could threaten to destroy the rest of her family. No - that too could backfire. His second glass was filling.

"Captain," Manny said. "Look what we found slinking around outside." The roughed-up body of a man tumbled across the floor before stopping in a heap at Woden's feet. He kicked the carcass. A metallic grin shadowed over his face. This wasn't a man. It was a vampire.

"Mijellin, my old friend," Woden said. "How nice of you to visit. I see you made long-distance space travel work for you. Good Job."

"Where is she?" he muttered. "Where is my Allaynie?"

"Tell me, do all of your kind cry valuable items?" Woden asked, ignoring the man's pleas to be reunited with his bride.

"What have you done with my wife?" Mijellin yelled, pushing himself into a kneeling position.

"Answer my questions and I will take you to her," Woden offered. "Do you all cry jewels?"

"No," Mijellin huffed. "Allaynie is special. Only golden vampires, the rarest of our kind, have that ability. Is that what this is all about - greed?"

"You call it greed. I call it business. We will have to agree to disagree on that point. Where can I find others like her?"

"I don't know," he answered, spitting out a mouthful of saliva mixed with blood. "I told you, they are rare. Vampires are not restricted to only our world. She was the only one from our planet. I can only tell you they always have royal blood."

"Do you all heal like she does?" Woden pried.

"Where is she?"

"My answers first," Woden yelled, slapping his latest prisoner across the face. "Or should we inflict serious injuries on you and wait for the results?"

"Yes and no," Mijellin answered. "We all heal, but Allaynie - golden vampires - have extra healing abilities."

"That's why it took you so long to attempt a rescue - the wounds we left you with needed time to heal. I see." The captain paced back to his glass. "Waste not, want not," he said, motioning cheers to the vampire before guzzling back the contents. "How many others came with you?"

"None," Mijellin answered. "I came alone."

"I don't believe you," Woden snarled. "What sort of a madman comes alone looking for a fight after having been defeated badly with home turf advantage?"

"Any man who loves his wife would," Mijellin answered.

"Love?" Woden laughed. "I have a wife. Love doesn't factor into it after the honeymoon is over. Oh ... that's right - you didn't have a honeymoon." Manny joined in the chorus of laughter.

Woden nodded to his lead hand. "Did you find his vessel?"

"We found a ship." Manny nodded. "It's too crude to be from around these parts. I'm not sure we could sell it even if we stripped it down for parts. It's all scrap metal, if you ask me."

"Scrap metal still has value," Woden replied. "Did you see anyone else?"

"Nah," Manny answered. "I doubt he could find anyone to join him on a suicide mission after the state we left him in."

"Still," Woden said. "She is royalty. Her father could have ordered it." He paused. "Take a few men and search the area around here - then head over to where you found his vessel and take a second look. Remember, they will still be sensitive to light and probably lurking in the shadows - if there any others."

"You said I could see Allaynie," Mijellin reminded.

"You will," Woden said, pouring another glass of whiskey - straight up this time, the ice cubes having melted. "When I am assured there is no further risk. Until then, you are my guest. Make yourself comfortable."

Mijellin fell on his face - the result of a steel-toed boot planted squarely in his back.

Laughter.

*****

"No sign of anyone else, Captain," Manny said. Keys clashed on the table. "We checked everywhere. I think he was telling the truth - crazy vamp."

Woden half-chuckled. Sometimes everything was too easy - handed to him for the taking. He had no problem accepting. These vampires may seem civilized on the outside, but they were as stupid as any other beast he hunted. In fact, some of his prey had been significantly more challenging to bring down. "Sammy, double time the men in both areas," Woden ordered. "Alright, let's go see your bride. Get him to his feet, but keep his hands bound. I don't want any situations to arise."

The metal door locked behind them. The only way out was through Samson on the other side. A distinct cellar odour grew stronger the further they descended - a damp rot and mold, mixed together into one scent.

A succession of snapping sounds and a step buckled under the weight of Mijellin's foot, sending it crashing through splintered wood. A familiar boot landed on his back, propelling his body forward, but leaving his foot behind. Woden sidestepped the falling vampire, laughing at his tumble.

"Been meaning to fix the stairs," the captain yelled. "Watch your step."

Mijellin winced at the pain. The small break away from his captors wasn't enough for him to recover from the fall. Manny's hands grabbed his shirt collar, pulling him to an upright position again. A rattle up ahead told him keys were opening another lock - followed by the creak of a door.

"Feel like making me some money today?" Woden asked.

Allaynie turned her back to him with no answer.

"I thought you might act this way," the captain said, his fingers caressing the cold steel iron bars that kept his trophy prisoner. "I brought you a surprise that might change your mind." He took a step backwards. "Bring him in."

Mijellin's body hurled across the floor landing in a heap against the cage. The sadness that had made its home in his eyes since the day they wed found the pain and anguish that lived in hers. "My love!" he cried.

"Mijellin!" she shrieked. "Why are you here?"

"He came to rescue his bride," Woden scoffed. "And a mighty fine job he's doing, too." His open hand slapped the vampire groom on the back. "Manny."

He didn't need any other words. His lead hand grabbed a fistful of hair, pulling Mijellin's head backwards. The same shiny blade that held him prisoner on their wedding day bit into his neck enough to release blood again.

"What are you doing?!" Allaynie screamed. "You promised you wouldn't kill him."

"And you promised to do as you're told. I don't see any tears."

Allaynie alternated her glance between all three men. Her hands gripped two bars. She dropped to her knees - broken. A tear streamed down her face, forming into diamond form before hitting the ground. "I will cry for you," she muttered.

"Yes, you will," Woden whispered through the bars.

A simple nod - the blade sliced through Mijellin's throat deep enough to ensure there was no return. Allaynie screamed.

"Cry me a river," Woden laughed.

Tears.

Chapter Seven

Allaynie held her eyes closed. The creak of the basement door meant someone was coming. It was too early for the arrangement of left overs her captors called a meal. She sighed - another beating was probably in the immediate future.

"Pst."

Th unusual noise made her look. Darn, they caught her off-guard now they knew she wasn't still knocked out from the last bout of brutality.

"Can you understand me?" a man asked, pronouncing each syllable clearly in slow motion. "We mean you no harm. We come in peace."

"What?"

"Good," he answered. "You speak some of our language."

"Get out of the way, Theon," Eva barked, knocking the man from his squatting position onto his backside. Her fingers traced the keyhole lock on the cell bars. "Stand back. We are going to have to use a little explosive on this."

A bang - then a puff of smoke.

"Come quickly," Eva said. "We're taking you someplace safe."

Someplace safe - did such a thing exist anymore? That ruthless man would hunt her to the ends of the universe and back again. Everything was a game to him - sacrificing lives in exchange for money and property - winning the only objective that mattered.

No words formed. Her feet moved quickly. The grip of the woman's hand around her wrist tightened, pulling her along. The man kept the pace from behind, sandwiching her - as if that could keep her safe.

"It's not much farther now," she huffed, her breath labouring.

A bang.

Allaynie glanced over her shoulder only long enough to see Theon fall to the ground motionless. She gasped. The hunt had begun.

A second bang.

Eva's grip released. Her mouth formed the word *run*, before she collapsed on the ground. Allaynie hurdled the body. Her speed increased, allowing the vampire part of her to stretch muscles that had been confined for too long. She heard more noises, but ignored them. As long as she had breath, she would continue to flee. Death would be welcomed. But deep inside, she knew the captain would never let her have such peace.

"Allaynie," a voice called. She sensed it before hearing it. It belonged to Bantil, the one whose offer for marriage she refused in favour of Mijellin. Self-preservation instincts took over - her body sped towards the voice.

She felt his arm link with hers - the pace of their steps synchronized. The door to a vessel opened directly in their path. He ushered her inside - the door clanging behind them.

"Mijellin?" he asked.

She shook her head twice before burying it in his chest.

"Go," Bantil ordered. "Put as much distance between us and this place as possible."

Chapter Eight

"What happened?" Woden asked.

"We missed her," one of his men answered.

"Obviously," Woden barked. "But how did this happen? And where is she now?"

"Gone."

"Gone," Woden repeated. "Vanished into thin air?" His hat came down hard, hitting the man square on the head.

"No sir," the man answered, trembling. "Best we can figure, these two were trying to help her escape. After they went down, she got fast - really fast. A ship was waiting for her. She boarded and it left."

"A ship," Woden said. "Manny, I thought you said there was no one around that hunk of junk."

"There wasn't, Captain," Manny answered. "That heap of junk is still right there." He pointed. "He must have brought it as a decoy. I guess the stiff wasn't as stupid as we thought."

"Idiots," Woden muttered. The toe of his shoe jabbed at the side of Eva's now stiffened body. Each kick becoming harder as if could add more injury to death. His eyes dilated, allowing darkness to overtake the light - opening a window to his soul. He huffed - his warm breath visible in the cool evening air. "Get them up. We can't leave them here." The light on the screen of his phone came to life. With a few clicks it rang. "Good evening, doctor," he said. "I have an emergency. I need you to meet me at your clinic."

"It's closed for the night," the man on the other end said.

"So open it," Woden ordered. "I'll be there in five." The light extinguished. "I want a team of men cleaning up this blood. Use a strong bleach. I don't want any traces left."

*****

The second body landed on the medical table with a thud. "What do you want me to do with these two?" Peters asked. "I don't want to be caught up in a scandal. Medical malpractice is all the rage at the moment. I don't need to tell you what bad press can do to a man's occupation."

"Then you shouldn't have asked me to hunt you down all those rare cuts of meat you love so much," Woden scoffed. "That would look even worse in the paper. I can see the headlines now, *Doctor Hires Poachers To Satisfy His Lust.*"

Blackmail.

"You wouldn't," the doctor said.

"Oh, I would," Woden barked back. "I'm calling in a favour. Once it's done, we never speak of it again. We'll be on par." A sharp needle attached to a hose caught his attention. "What's this for?"

"It drains blood - mainly used for autopsies."

"Can you use two at once?" Woden asked, a luster returning to his eyes.

"I suppose - although I'm not sure why you would want to," the doctor replied. "One does the job fine. Can we get back to the issues at hand?" His hand alternated motioning between the two bodies. "What is it you want me to do with them?"

"I have a plan that will solve everyone's problems and keep both our names clear of falling from grace. If anything, this will make you famous." He placed two fingers on the neck of the reporter. "I want you to use two of those things and drain the blood from right here. When you are done, I will need pictures. The neck should be documented in your reports as the spot from which the blood was completely drained from the body."

"I'm not following you."

"Positioned correctly, isn't it possible that two sharp teeth could make the puncture wounds?" Wooden asked.

"I suppose," the doctor answered. "But what creature would do such a thing? I know of nothing local capable of leaving such a mark, let alone draining all of the blood from a body. There are reports of a bat to the south, but they prefer the big toe. I actually have been thinking about taking a trip to investigate those little suckers." He chuckled at his own joke.

"Vampires," Woden hissed. "They drink the blood of their prey. Try to stay on-topic. I don't have the time or the patience to listen to your ramblings about your next family vacation."

"I can't suggest something so outlandish," the doctor snarled. "I'd be the laughing stock of my profession."

"I didn't ask you to," Woden barked back. "I'll take care of the details. You just make it look possible. If asked, the cause of the punctures are unknown but consistent with a possible bite pattern."

"What about the gunshots - other doctors are sure to notice." Peters argued. He always knew Woden was eccentric, but this was verging on madness.

"Hide them," Woden answered. "I don't want any signs of trauma other than the two puncture marks. A little makeup should do. I'll be calling in a favour at the crematorium. When your report is done, ship them over there."

"There will be questions," Peters said, shaking his head. "We'll be accused of tampering with evidence in a murder. There is no way we will get away with this."

"Did you know a vampire's bite can change an ordinary person into a vampire themselves?" Woden asked.

"No. I didn't," the doctor said, backing away from the table. "Can it?"

"Oh yes," Woden replied. "When the sun sets on the evening following the bite, the dead rise again. Not as the same person mind you, instead they come back as something much worse - a vampire themselves - a soulless creature. The only way to stop them, in this in between stage, is by burning their bodies to ash. We don't have much time. If one vampire bites two people and they bite two people - well, you can do that math."

The doctor twitched, trying to hide the shivers running down his spine, the goosebumps on his arms revealing his secret. "You've seen this drinking of the blood?"

Rational thought loses its meaning when standing before the gates of fear. Take the good doctor, for instance - he no longer realized the two victims had been shot, not bitten.

"Yes," Woden answered. "All my men have seen them suck blood from the neck of another. They are beasts, doctor. I am going to hunt her down in the name of justice - if it's the last thing I do."

"Fine," Peters said. "I'll do it. You handle the details and press. I want my name kept low-key, in case the whole thing blows up. I'll start with the man." He paused. "Isn't this your son?"

"Yes," Woden answered. "Unfortunate set of circumstances. He should have listened to his horoscope and stayed home today."

The doctor glanced up from the man's neck. "Woden, he's still alive."

"That's a stroke of luck," the captain said. The corners of his lips quivered slightly as they turned upwards.

"I'd say." The doctor answered.

"The puncture marks will be much more realistic," Woden laughed.

"Good God," Peters cried. "He's your son. You actually want me to kill him? With a pint of blood, I could save him."

"It's us or him. If I go down, I won't be going alone." Woden stated. "And I appreciate the sacrifice Theon is making. I doubt his brothers would have done so well."

A white cloth dabbed the perspiration from the doctor's brow. He hung his head, weighing his options. The urge to run for the door subsided with the realization he would be dead before he left the building. The man standing before him was ruthless.

"Don't get all confused over morality on me now," Woden said. "It never bothered you to eat the flesh of endangered beasts, extinguishing their existence - this shouldn't bother you either."

"It's not the same," Peters muttered.

"It's exactly the same. We are all animals - nothing more," Woden yelled. "Remember, there is still a chance he will die and rise as a vampire." He circled the steel tables, pacing. His fist smashed down on a tray, sending a few sterile instruments flying. "And keep your gods out of it. This has nothing to do with any of them. If they had any concern for people at all, they would strike a bolt of lightning through everyone of those vampire beasts. The heads of religions wonder why their followings have been steadily declining. But then again..."

His words cut off. "Make sure this is done quickly." Woden fumbled in the drawer of a nearby desk, finally pulling out a pen. A pink memo notepad quickly filled up with inked scratchings. "That's the name of the crematorium. They will be expecting the bodies. Be a good man and make sure they are delivered in a timely fashion."

"If I do this," the doctor said. "You never bother me again."

"If you do this," Woden replied. "I won't have to."

The wheels turn - a new plan.

Chapter Nine

He sighed. That church was the least favourite place he could imagine visiting. It was also the last place he shed a tear. A tear that came from abuse - abuse at the hands of his own mother. He huffed at the word. She had no right to be called that.

Woden mused at the situation. The man for whom tears didn't fall, forcing a vampire to cry him a fortune. That was *irony*. If there was one thing the old hag taught him, it was how to make tears flow. He chuckled. Perhaps he should be thanking her for that. He froze at the open doors for several moments.

It was vampires who shouldn't be able to enter, not a man.

The evening service was already underway. Voices of praise pushed him back. He stumbled down a couple of steps. Resolve etched itself onto the face of the man. What was he afraid of - bursting into flames? If that was going to happen, it would have when his mother dragged him inside years ago. He could still hear the shrill screams - demon - devil - beast.

He'd spent his whole life trying to live up to it.

*****

Woden shifted his weight several times attempting to awaken those parts of him that fell asleep during the sermon - surprisingly, that didn't include his mind. The old-fashioned wooden pews weren't made for comfort. Adding to the discomfort was the stand; sit; kneel; sit; stand, format of the service. It was enough to make the lower half of any man take a hiatus. Attendance being as low as it was, the church should have invested a bit of cash into cushions at least.

The last row was his preferred seating in any house of worship - not that it mattered, there were only two other people in attendance for the evening ritual. A low snore told him at least one of the other two chose dreamland over the long-winded speech about morality.

The slight dip in the bench played havoc on his back. He rotated his neck to compensate. The state of his shoulders felt better, but a dull ache still resonated from the bottom of his spine upwards.

A heaviness in his chest reminded him that this service couldn't end soon enough. A wave of sickness hit him, knocking all the air from is body. He tried inhaling deep breaths and was rewarded with nausea.

Keep breathing.

Tired of listening to the ramblings of a man, he considered less than qualified to preach, Woden turned his attention to the building's architecture and art. Images adorned every empty space possible - all of a mortal version of god. He chuckled under his breath. Religion - every world he visited had at least one and, in some cases, many different types. They all sounded the same - hypocritical. Gods with their message of love, peace and goodwill and their followers who kill others to spread that message. There was only one god he would believe in - himself. At least he was reliable enough to always show up. The corner of his eye caught a glimpse of the other two patrons exiting.

"Hello, Father," Woden said, approaching the front. Years had passed. If this priest was truly a holy man, he would remember.

"What a surprise to see you here," the priest said. "Have you come to save your soul before the day of judgement is upon you?"

The day of judgement had already come.

"No, nothing that extreme," Woden said. "I came to save you."

"Save me?" the priest smiled.

"More to the point, to save your religion," Woden proclaimed. The brim of his hat circled around in his fingers as he spoke. "I would like to help you boost your attendance."

"Now why would a man such as yourself do that for me?" the priest asked. "Feeling a bit nostalgic?"

Selling one's soul to the devil wasn't the common practice of those bound to the church. He first met Woden when he was a wee lad. There was no other way to describe him than a bit of a handful - the one trouble always had a way of finding.

The day his mother dragged him in, claiming the number *666* was engraved on his scalp, was as vivid as if it happened only yesterday. She refused to keep him any longer - screaming that her son was a demon - a beast that needed to be destroyed. She begged for the church to intervene in the name of God now, before someone needed to hunt him down later.

The physical abuse Woden suffered was severe. The nasty scars on his forearms, left from being branded by various religious objects, was proof of that. The mental scars were worse. Foster parents and group homes didn't help the situation. He bounced around between them for a while before disappearing as a teen. Somewhere in his mid-twenties he resurfaced.

"I believe we have a common enemy," Woden explained. "It isn't only your religion. I already have others from multiple worlds lined up. This is an invitation to jump on the bandwagon, so to speak. I wouldn't even offer if it weren't for what you did for me when I was younger. I don't have fond memories of this place - as I am sure you are aware."

"A common enemy - sounds fascinating," the priest said. The smell of burning wax and soot encompassed them for a moment, before rising with traces of smoke as the only reminders of lit candles from the service. "Please continue."

"My eldest son was murdered earlier," Woden offered.

A new trap baited - waiting for prey.

"My dear man," the priest said, falling into Woden's net. "I had no idea you were under such emotional duress. If I can do anything to alleviate your pain, say the word. Together we can pray for your son's soul."

"That's the problem, Father," Woden said. "It's too late for his soul."

"Nonsense," the priest replied. "God is forgiving to all those who need forgiveness. My door has always been open to you and your family, to help you find your way."

"It isn't that simple. My son was killed by a demon - a devil in its evilest form."

"A demon," the priest said. "Sometimes a man can seem like he is such a thing. The act of murder is the devil's work."

"No," Woden said. "An actual demon - a vampire. She fed off him - draining every last drop of his blood."

"How?"

"Vampires have two fangs that they use to pierce the skin - penetrating directly into a vein," Woden explained. "After death, the corpse takes a new life - coming back as a demon. A new vampire is born without any attachment to its previous life."

"You're serious," the priest replied.

"Very," Woden answered. "Right now the only things we know affect them are fire and being pierced through the heart. Sunlight has some effect on them as well."

"So where do I fit in?"

"These abominations go against the glory of your god," Woden answered. "I would expect certain religious items would have a profound effect on the demons. They would offer a certain level of protection against them."

"I'm afraid science is what you need to back you," the priest said, resuming extinguishing candles. "Not the church."

"I have science already," Woden said. "There are doctor reports substantiating my claims. I am offering you a chance to rebuild your congregation. When word gets out about demons walking amongst us, the people will need guidance - spiritual guidance. You could be the one to offer that to them. All I ask is a few blessed items and a portion of your collection to support the destruction of the evil. If you aren't interested, say the word and I will be on my way. There are enough other religions willing to put an end to the devil's plans."

"How much of the collection?"

"Let's say fifty percent," Woden answered.

"Fifty?" the priest asked, shaking his head.

"Fine, forty - keep in mind a full service with sixty percent of the collection is much better than one hundred percent of two people," Woden replied.

"You'll be mentioning our support in your demon hunt to the press, I assume?" the priest asked. How ironic, the man whose own mother called him a demon, wanted to become a demon hunter.

"Yes," Woden said.

"We cannot have the church recognized as participating in the hunt," the priest said. "You'll need a new name. How about instead of hunters, you take on the role of Purifiers?"

"An excellent suggestion," Woden replied. "Purifiers sanctioned by the church it is." He extended his hand to seal the deal.

The priest accepted - he knew they were all the same.

Trophy acquired.

Chapter Ten

"I don't see why we need to attend this press conference," Detective Fumie said. "We've been slapped on the hands and told not to interfere."

"Woden has the backing of nine out of ten religions," Detective Tanner answered. "No politician is going to allow us to go against the word of any god in an election year. That man has luck shoved where the sun don't shine. I still want to hear what he has to say. If we are going to be fighting demons, we will need to know how."

"I suppose," Fumie answered, grabbing a plain black jacket off her chair. "Do you really buy into it all? Vampires and demons, I mean."

"That's what I'm hoping to find out." He swung his tan coloured jacket over his shoulder. "Be prepared. It's going to be a nut farm out there." He tossed her a cross on a chain. "It might come in handy. I hear demons don't like God."

"They probably don't like guns either," she smirked. "I heard silver bullets do wonders for ripping apart their flesh and blowing them back through the gates of hell."

"That's a werewolf," her partner scoffed. "Didn't you watch that new show the other night? The wife hasn't stopped going on about it." He sipped coffee from the hole in his travel mug. "You need to get your monsters straight."

"What are you hoping to find?" she answered. "This isn't about the creep-show. You've been my partner for a long time. What gives?"

"The year I first graduated from the academy," he explained. "I was called to a routine, apparent heart attack. There was something not quite right about the death. She was mentally ill and lived alone. Along came Woden - out of nowhere. I mean there hadn't been any sign of him for years, but he popped up the same day as his estranged mother's death. I heard the word coincidence far too many times during that investigation. Dr. Peters examined the body and listed the cause of death as a massive coronary. Of course, with Woden the only kin, no autopsy was performed."

"I hate to have to agree," Fumie started. She found a file in her hand before she could finish. "What's this?"

"Take a look at the medical reports," Tanner suggested.

"Doctor Peters," she mumbled.

"You and I both know too many coincidences add up to foul play," Tanner said.

"Even if it does," Fumie replied. "We've been ordered off the case. We can't touch him with all the hype."

"I know," Tanner stated. "But when he does mess up and falls from grace, I want to be there to catch him and any accomplices he had along the way."

She nodded her head, extending her arm towards her partner for a fist bump. He laughed, leaving her hanging.

Chapter Eleven

The constant flashing of cameras trying to snap the perfect picture was enough to give anyone a headache. The top from a white bottle of pain killers popped off, landing on the ground. Woden tipped the remaining contents into his mouth and dry swallowed. The bottle settled beside its lid. He shoved his hand in his pocket retrieving the small white button. It flipped in the air indicating the start to a game of heads or tails - a game he couldn't lose.

Reporters, from every planet capable of space travel in the light side of the universe, formed rows around a podium. A constant hum of chatter enveloped the area. The words of one mixing with the words of others, resulting in an overabundance of garbled noise.

"Ahem." The microphone vibrated the clearing of Woden's voice - the clamour loud enough to gather attention.

Silence.

"I'd like to say good morning," Woden said. "But, under the circumstances, I cannot. I am sure many of you have heard the rumours of my son's death. I am here to confirm those details."

A wave of rumblings.

"If you could keep your questions and comments to the end, I promise I will do my best to answer everyone," Woden offered. "Copies of medical reports are being passed out as I speak. The contents are consistent with a vampire attack. I submit these soulless creatures are the root of evil. Every religion we know of has agreed to commission a task force of Purifiers to rid our communities of these demons. I will personally be in charge. You have my vow to protect."

News - the fastest way to spread fear and hate.

Journalists circled like vultures - thinking they were somehow doing their world a service. In reality, all they do is play into the hands men with well-constructed plans. Within days, reports would flow to his ears with sightings of anything suspicious. It didn't matter how far Allaynie ran, now, he would find her.

"Donations are being accepted," Woden bellowed. "The sooner we have funding, the sooner we can embark on this holy crusade."

*****

"Nice speech, Cap'n," Manny said.

"How are the donations?" Woden asked, his fingers fumbling through loose bills littering their worktable.

"We almost have enough to pick up the supplies we need," Manny answered. "Money is flowing in - to fight evil."

"Good," Woden answered. "I want to start as soon as possible. Send some men to pick up our religious supplies and load them. I've asked for stakes to pierce their hearts and silver bullets."

"Isn't that going a bit overboard?" Manny asked.

"I don't think so," Woden replied. "The more sensational it is, the more fear it creates. That translates into cold, hard cash for us."

"I agree with you there," Manny said. "It's those skeptics I am worried about. There is already one claiming to know a vampire who isn't evil."

"If that person met an untimely end at the fangs of a vampire," Woden suggested, "it would strengthen our position. Have a team take care of it." He threw a business card on the table. "We have our own doctor to handle such cases now. While you are at it, best take care of Peters too. He knows too much for his own good. Let news of the deaths leak to all the right sources."

"I like the way you think," Manny said. "Makes me proud to serve under your command."

"Has she surfaced?"

"No, Cap'n, not yet." Manny answered. "But she will. There won't be a nook or cranny left to hide in soon."

"Yes," Woden said. "But we have to start our journey somewhere."

"What about the girl's home?" Manny suggested. "She may have headed there."

"Perhaps," Woden replied. "Regardless, we can destroy her world. As soon as a couple of ships are packed, send them to wipe out her clan."

"Kill 'em all?"

"Every last one," Woden replied. "We can send a team to pillage anything of value after. I plan to erase the vampire race from existence, except for a select few of the golden."

Chapter Twelve

"Cap'n."

"Ah," Woden muttered, pushing away bits of glass with his hand. He blinked a few times before scratching his head and sitting up. Blood trickled onto what was once a white undershirt, now yellowed with sweat, from a wound on the back of his shoulder - still impaled by a large sliver of the bottle he had been drinking when he passed out. He pulled it out, cutting his hand in the process. His tongue licked the blood from his fingers. He chuckled. Drinking blood wasn't exclusive to vampires after all.

He winced with every move. With all the advances man had made, they still couldn't put carpeting in a ship. He rolled onto his knees, clenching his teeth at the feeling of cement floors battling with his joints and winning. Bottles clashed together, giving way to the weight of his staggering stance.

"There ya are," Woden said, one eye closed. His fist grasped at air a few times before closing around the white pill container. A bottle crashed to the ground - its shards sharing space with the one from the previous evening. He lifted another, emptying a few drops into his mouth. Curses in every language burst from his quivering lips until the contents of a single bottle provided enough for a mouthful. He gargled the spirits then poured in a few painkillers and swallowed. A nasal sound of phlegm escaped from his throat - followed by a deep hacking cough.

"Cap'n," Manny repeated.

"What is it," he slurred in a raspy voice.

"I don't want to upset you," Manny said. "But I thought you should know, our numbers are dwindling."

He sighed, stumbling into a seat. "Those vampires have taken out far too many of us. Lives are the price we pay for victory at war."

"Yes," Manny said. "We have had large losses, but more and more men are returning home. There hasn't been a vampire sighting on our side of the universe in over a year now."

"Deserters," Woden snarled. Crimson red appeared in the spittle that dropped to the table from his mouth. "They are just as bad as the vampires. We have taken the lives of just as many vampires, if not more. Is that not an accomplishment to be proud of?"

"It is. Perhaps, we have already won. Like I said, there hasn't been a vampire sighting in over a year now," Manny repeated. "At least on our side of the universe. We can't maintain a fight moving further into the dark zone. There are too many unknown variables - not to mention creatures more frightening than vampires."

"Are you a coward?" Woden yelled, phlegm riddled with red and brown specks projected with his words.

"No, Cap'n," Manny said. "But your health is faltering. Why not return home a hero now? You could live a comfortable life with what you have left. Income is drying up. Vampires and monsters that go bump in the night are becoming nothing more than myths. No one cares anymore."

"I care!" Woden screamed, his breath wheezing. The coughing intervals were too close together as of late to bother trying to cover his mouth. "You are asking me to give up the hunt."

"Yes, Cap'n - I am," Manny said. "It's been years since your family has seen you. Don't you want to spend the time you have left with them?"

"I won't let her win," he replied. "Be gone with ya. Don't disturb me until you have a confirmed sighting."

Family - he chuckled at the thought.

*****

"Cap'n," Manny said, peeking in from a crack in the door. "I know you said not to disturb you, but you haven't come out in days." He swatted at a couple of flies trying to escape the confines of the room. His hand knocked the door open further - a whiff of rot drifted out. "You might want to give yourself a wash Cap'n."

Silence.

"Cap'n," Manny repeated, pushing the door fully open. He covered his nose with his shirt - more odours leaked out. He shook his head. He didn't need to go any closer to know his captain had passed on, but out of respect, he did. A sheet fell over the Woden's lifeless stare. The grim reaper's touch tickled a smile onto his face that only decomposition would erase.

Manny pried an envelope from his grasp with the word *Blaine* written on it - his eldest living son. How ironic his lead hand should shed a single tear for him, much the same as Allaynie had for Mijellin the day of her escape.

In the end, death is the only winner.

Chapter Thirteen

"Do you think the charges will stick?" Fumie asked her partner.

"Yeah," Tanner answered. "We have him. He won't be able to talk his way out of his one."

The ship landed without incident. "Just the one door on this model vessel." Detective Fumie surveyed the situation. Catching Woden was the mission, but the safety of those under her command the priority. "Franklin," she yelled. "Split into two teams. I want both sides of that door covered."

The squeaking sound of rusted metal indicated the door was opening. "Look alive!" Tanner yelled. "They're coming out."

Manny side-eyed the officers bordering the ramp as he descended. The hero's welcome anticipated was non-existent. Instinctively, he put his hands in the air.

"On the ground," Franklin ordered.

Manny complied. It was over. None of the skeleton crew would risk further loss of life. Their allegiance to Woden died with him.

"Where is he?" Tanner yelled.

Courage can't be measured by the size of the package it comes in. A click beside Samson's ear was enough to make the silent, strong man squeal. "I'll tell you what you want to know."

"Where is he?" Tanner yelled again, pushing the barrel of a gun into Samson's cheek. "Where is Woden?"

"He's dead!" Sammy screamed.

"You'll find his body in the captain's quarters," Manny added. "He must have passed away in his sleep. I covered him with a sheet, but couldn't do anything about the stench."

Fumie nodded to the officers to investigate. Her weapon already secured in its holster, she grabbed a pair of handcuffs from her back pocket.

"He's dead," Franklin confirmed.

"Secure the vessel," Tanner snarled. "'ll send for a medical examiner."

Woden managed to slip through their fingers once again. Escaping the justice of this world hopefully meant penance in the afterlife.

*****

He would have given anything for a cool glass of water and a cloth to wipe the sweat streaming down his face. "I always thought those lights were just for show in the movies - never would have guessed the police used 'em in real investigations," Manny snickered. "I hope this isn't going to be a good cop, bad cop routine as well."

Detective Tanner pulled a chair up beside him, smiling at the man's eyes watching the drops of condensation on the can of a cold soda pop. The tab popped. He guzzled the contents in one breath. "Ah," he moaned. "Refreshing. I bet you'd like one. Why don't you tell me what happened?"

"He died."

"Just like that," Tanner said. "He died overnight?"

"He'd been sick for a while," Manny said. "I told him it was time to retire - spend a bit of time with the family while he could."

"But he didn't listen?"

"No sir," Manny answered. "He was set on saving the world from vampires. If he hadn't passed on, we'd still be out there."

"I bet that made you mad," Tanner smirked.

"No sir," Manny answered. "I was with him through thick and thin."

"Tell me about Doctor Peters?"

"The doctor was a client," Manny offered. "He had a pallet for unusual meat."

"Who killed him?"

"He's dead?" Manny asked. "Sorry to hear. I don't mean to be rude, but isn't it your job to find out who killed him if it was murder?"

"Don't play innocent!" Tanner yelled. "The good doctor took the liberty of leaving a journal in case something happened to him. He was afraid of Woden."

"Lots of folks were afraid of Woden," Manny replied. "He wasn't a saint. If he killed the doctor, he took it with him to the grave."

Tanner opened a file folder, fetching an envelope from within. "Who's Blaine?" He asked, sliding it across the table.

"That would be Woden's son," Manny answered. "I pried that from his hand when I found him. I was planning to deliver it."

"Do you know what it says?" the detective asked.

"No," Manny answered. "I have no business poking my nose into another man's family life. Whatever he wrote was for his son's eyes only."

"Mind if I open it?"

"I doubt how I feel will have any bearing on what you decide." Manny barely had time to finish his sentence before the envelope ripped.

The frown lines on Tanner's face deepened. "It's your legacy - WIN," he read. "What does that mean? Is it some sort of code?"

"I have no idea," Manny retorted. "You'd have to ask his son."

"You sticking with the story that vampires are to blame?" the detective asked.

"Vampires, like it or not, are very real," Manny explained. "I have seen them. They are out there. You may have your issues with Woden, but he did a service to men."

"A service?" Tanner scoffed.

"Aye," Manny said. "He gave us a chance to be prepared. Before you discredit him, ask yourself what happens when they return."

"By they, you mean vampires."

"I do," Manny answered. "If people don't believe, they will be left defenceless. Some trade-offs are the best thing for the universe."

Tanner's chair slammed against the table.

"You don't buy it - do you?" Fumie asked, waiting on the other side of the interrogation room door. "He's got to be lying."

"They all have the same story," Tanner answered. "Looks like we have a few more unsolved cases. We'll need a room in the basement to store them all in if this keeps up. Cut 'em loose."

"Loose, sir?" Franklin asked. "I know I'm still a rookie, but what about the autopsy reports? The doctor's findings are consistent with poisoning."

"Yes," Tanner said. "They are also consistent with a half dozen diseases. I have no intention of spending taxpayer money to find out the man had heart disease."

"There were traces of chemicals on some of the bottles found in his room," the rookie said.

"Coincidence."

"The men were tired and wanted to come home," Franklin pestered, following the detective to his desk. "Each one admitted they wouldn't be able to as long as Woden lived. That's motive."

"Coincidence," Tanner uttered. He motioned to a tall pile of files resting on his desk. "These are already collecting dust. There are other crimes that need our attention."

"Something doesn't feel right, sir," Franklin commented.

"Do me a favour and deliver this envelope to Woden's son. You can take over the body release forms to his family at the same time," he said. A part of him felt sorry for the officer. He knew from experience that this case would haunt him for years to come. *What ifs* were a cop's biggest bane. His gaze didn't falter from paperwork until after the young officer took his leave.

"I thought you wanted to nail that creep," Fumie said.

"He's dead," Tanner answered. "I can't do much to him now. It's out of my reach. I'm sure there is a price he is paying for whatever crimes he committed in this life."

"What about justice for the families of his victims?" Fumie asked.

"Justice? I think it was served."

Coincidence - he finally understood the deeper meaning of the word.

Chapter Fourteen

Over time, tales of vampires and other creatures from shapeshifters to lizard men became nothing more than myths. The dark part of the universe where monsters dwell was soon forgotten. It was easier not to acknowledge something rather than to live in fear. Generations passed. Words became whispers. Time erased space - leaving behind footprints that someone's shoes would one day fill again.

The damage to the vampire race was irreversible. They would forever be known as soulless demons, capable only of murder - a race enslaved by evil. For them, there was no choice but to evolve. Their survival depended on it.

They soon learnt suppressing the vampire part of them came easy. Emotions were the key. To control one's own demons, one must first master control of his or her own feelings.

It was a new era. Vampires blended into society, never letting anyone in on their secrets, not even the closest of friends. Fear of persecution and annihilation made them keep the silence. Before long, it wasn't even questioned anymore. This was the life of a vampire - cursed to hide in the shadows from those who would hunt them. Even in the solitude of their own kingdoms, the mask of *normal* was always donned.

The word purifier wasn't heard again - until last week. The reports of the brutal murder of young girl at the hands of this hunter group shook the core of the vampire community.

*****

"Your father is contacting as many worlds as he can to warn them of the possible danger," the man said. "That's why he couldn't come with you."

"I know," she whispered, her mind still processing the story she had been told. "He's always done what is best for me."

Destiny. Could two separate individuals mirror each other's lives so closely that they were fated to walk the exact same path?

"What happened to Allaynie?" Tomoiya asked.

"There is no record of that," the man answered. "Vampires do not age as quickly as men. Where Woden's body grew weak, Allaynie would have lived on. I would imagine she settled down somewhere and quite possibly is still hiding."

"The man is dead, though," Tomoiya said.

"Yes," the man answered. "He is dead. There are many races in existence. Men are not the only ones affected by gold fever. Trusting anyone other than another vampire can be a mistake. Do you know why your mother wanted you to have this book?"

"Because I liked it so much," Tomoiya answered.

"Partly," the man said. "There are similarities between you and Allaynie. I am sure you have noticed at least one or two."

Tomoiya's eyes flashed golden then returned to their usual milk-chocolate brown colour.

The man chuckled. "That is the big one. It is said the fate of the golden vampires are linked - somehow intertwined. Your mother wanted you to know the good part of Allaynie's life. She wanted you to understand that you too can find happiness. Remember, doom spelled backwards is mood. That is something you can control."

"Why didn't she tell me the rest of the story?" Tomoiya asked. "Why did she keep it from me?"

"No mother wants their child to worry," he answered. "It's time now for vigilance. You are going to be alone for a while and even with all the combat training I have given you, there will still be some dangers. Trust your instincts - they won't lead you astray. Most importantly, don't let the vampire side of you surface in front of strangers, if at all possible."

"How is coming here better than remaining at home? Am I not leaving one threat to go to another?" Saying goodbye to her home made less sense than before.

"Unfortunately, that is the life of a golden vampire," he said. "You are safe with your own kind. Even the shadiest vampire wouldn't harm something as beautiful and rare as you. This part of the universe is dominated by vampires. It is the other races who also dwell here that could prove dangerous. At the school you are going to be attending, no one exposes their alter ego. You won't know what race they are and they won't know you're a vampire. Keep it that way. The system has been successful for generations, ensuring no one race is persecuted."

"You won't be able to help me, will you?" she asked. He had been with her since birth - the general of her personal fleet.

"You'll be fine," the general said. "We have been preparing your skills for years for this exact moment. I have taught you all you need to know. If you need help, seek out the other vampires. We are a loyal race. They will stand by your side. I doubt it will come to that. Once your father has investigated these new purifiers, I am sure you will be able to go home."

A package wrapped in brown paper fell onto her lap. "What's this?" she asked.

"A gift from your father," he answered. "I have duties to attend to. Make sure you get some rest. Starting out in a new place as a sleepyhead isn't fun."

He didn't have to add the sleepyhead part to that statement. Having nothing familiar and no friends wasn't fun. The brown paper crinkled under the strain of her fingers. Giving up on opening it neatly, she ripped the wrapping into bits. Her hand smoothed over the cover of the journal that hid inside.

She held the two books up side-by-side. Except for age, they were identical. She placed Allaynie's Story on the table beside her. Its time in her life had come to an end. It took a few moments before she found the courage to open her new book. The blank pages inside invited her to fill them with all her emotions. She smiled, wiping a tear from the corner of her eye before it had the chance to form a diamond.

A blanket tossed up in the air, landing over her when it came back down. She wiggled her toes tucking them into warmth. The chair reclined. Held tightly against her chest was her new favourite book.

The general was right. He was always right. She was tired and needed rest. She closed her eyes. Sleep would come quickly. Her mind was at ease - content with the knowledge that morning would bring a new chapter in her life. Tomorrow she would start Tomoiya's story.

Author's Message

I hope you enjoyed reading *Escape to Darkness* as much as I did writing it. Watch for new books in this series in 2017.

Tomoiya's Story: Stalked

A new generation of purifiers surfaces, threatening Tomoiya's safety. Her father, the ruler of the Galaxy of the Thirteen Stars, sends her into hiding in the dark side of the universe. When rival races wage war against each other, Tomoiya's life is again at risk. Is there anywhere safe for a golden vampiric princess?

Other titles coming soon from C.A. King

Shattering the Effect of Time

Join the Shinning brothers, Jessie, Dezi and Pete as they set out on a quest to save their younger sister. No magic known to them or their friends has ever been able to reverse the grip of time. A few legends, however, exist mentioning ancient items that may hold the key to do exactly that.

This brand new series will take you on a search for the fountain of youth and mermaids; a quest for the holy grail; a trip to visit Daryl the mountain guru, in the hunt for the Cinamani Stone; on a search for ambrosia, the food of the gods; and other adventures.

Surviving the Sins

The prophecies are being rewritten. This time someone is using the seven deadly sins: Lust; Gluttony; Greed; Sloth; Wrath; Envy; and Pride, to unlock an ancient evil. The book falls into Jade's hands to answer destiny's call. Can she survive the sins?

The Portal Prophecies

These great titles in C.A. King's The Portal Prophecies series are available now at most online book retailers:

A Keeper's Destiny

A Halloween's Curse

Frost Bitten

Sleeping Sands

Deadly Perceptions

Finding Balance

The prophecies are the key to their survival. Can they solve them in time?